ROAD RAGER
DARK DRIVERS

This Book Belongs to:

CLANDESTINE ACTION AGENT

SECURITY CLEARANCE LEVEL: ALPHA

Road Rager: Dark Drivers

An ACTIONOPOLIS Book

Presented by Agent of D.A.N.G.E.R.

AGENT OF DANGER

KOMIKWERKS

Published by Komikwerks, LLC
1 Ruth Street
Worcester, MA 01602

Cover illustration by Leno Carvalho
Edited by Shannon Eric Denton
Book Design by Kristen Fitzner Denton

ISBN-13: 978-1-933925-61-5
ISBN: 1-933925-61-2

When Adventure Is Your Destination!

Dedication

For all the young heroes-in-training out there, patiently waiting for their super powers to kick in. Be patient. Your time will come.

— E.M.E.

TABLE OF CONTENTS

By Eric M. Esquivel

Created by

Shannon Eric Denton

and Eric M. Esquivel

When Adventure Is Your Destination!

PROLOGUE

Staying still for too long made Flynn Friedrich's blood boil. It gave him too much time to ruminate about all the things in life that he couldn't race away from, no matter how fast he got his tires to spin... like Krystal Lassiter, the new girl at school with the pretty green eyes and the infuriating laugh who mocked him relentlessly for the way he spent his nights.

"Racing? So, what—you just drive around in circles all day? It's weird they call that a sport... doesn't the car do all of the work

Yeah, and Leonardo Da Vinci just tossed pigment around. His paintbrush did all of the heavy lifting. As if.

It was a dumb thing to say, and she was a dork for even thinking it—but for some reason Flynn couldn't shake her from his thoughts. He hoped he'd get a chance to see her later and finish their argument— but first he had a race to win....regardless of her opinion on the matter.

"Gentlemen...start your engines!"

Something came over Flynn when he was behind the steering wheel of Big Daddy (the hot rod he built by himself, one bolt at a time, one hour at a time, utilizing information he had gleaned from hours and hours of online tutorials and countless overdue library books)—a zen-like state, a sort of gnostic burst of insight that made everything seem clear. For a lot of other drivers, racing was just a noisy distraction from their lives. For Flynn, his life was the noisy distraction from racing...

"Ready...set...GO!"

CHAPTER ONE

Drescher didn't know much about anything—but there were two things of which he was crystal clear:

One: A real man rides a motorcycle – and not one of those foreign jobs, either, a true-blue riding machine forged of American steel.

Two: That babbling old bag of bones was going to finish making with the mumbo jumbo, or Drescher and his boys were going to run the geezer down like he was just another hunk of roadkill too dumb to get outta their way.

Drescher and his gang were called "The Dark Drivers". They talked a lot of smack—a lot of smack—but at their core they were just another bored collection of good-for-nothing local ruffians who had exhausted the novelty of vandalism and illicit substances and had momentarily turned their attention to the blackest of magicks.

The Dark Drivers weren't spiritualists, they weren't of a particularly philosophical bent, and they sure as heck weren't Dungeons and Dragons aficionados—but they were lazy. If there was a pill they could take to simulate a state of mind, if there was a way they could cheat their way to a good grade without having to study, if there was a way they could steal something without having to earn it, they were game for it—no matter the long-term cost.

If magick was real, and all it took to make their dark dreams come true was to utter a couple of phrases in Latin and wave some old chicken bones around, then Drescher and his crew were one hundred and ten percent in. Who cares if it cost them their immortal souls? Odds are mighty good that they weren't gonna get past St. Peter anyway...

Their first attempts were pretty pedestrian: some animal sacrifices, minor graveyard desecrations, a few church fires, playing some heavy metal records backwards at midnight—the kind of macabre, predictable garbage one could expect from a bunch of black-denim-clad, suburban delinquents with a library card and a passing familiarity with scary movies and heavy metal.

It wasn't until Drescher stumbled upon Lassiter—an elderly vagrant completely-out-of-his-mind by all counts, who hung out behind the local watering hole and claimed (among many other things) to be a "master of the mystic arts" who could "peel back the veil between the quotidian world and expose the deepest, darkest secrets of The Realms Beyond" (for a dollar fifty)—that Drescher and the rest of the Dark Drivers started messing around with the real occult.

During their first meeting, for a couple cans of cheap beer, Lassiter explained to Drescher and the Dark Drivers the big secret of the universe (that is wasn't really a "universe" at all, but more like a "polyverse" of overlapping realities crammed full of different "gods", citizens, rules of physics—all of which could be bargained with, if one was so inclined). The next night, for a box of wine, he showed them how to project their bleakest thoughts and cloud the minds of men. On the third, Lassiter showed them something even more shocking: his long forgotten backbone.

Lassiter was in a rare, sober (despite his best efforts earlier in the day) state that night, and the clarity of mind that the once-in-a-blue-moon state afforded him caused him to remember why he started drinking heavily in the first place: to forget about all of this malarkey. To put the terrible things that he had seen when he was young and dumb and intent on self-destruction out of his mind, and in the past where they belong.

Lassiter figured that, much like the ancient history he was running from, there wasn't much he could do about the mistakes—except make dang sure not to make them ever again. So that's what he did. He politely refused the rowdy young men's offering of cold ones and cash and attempted to inconspicuously sulk into the shadows before they could interrogate him further.

The Dark Drivers weren't big fans of subtlety. And they were even less fond of things not going exactly as they'd like. When Lassiter refused to show them anything else the Dark Drivers lost their collective minds with entitled rage. Drescher, quickest to anger, was the first to speak up:

"What do you mean you won't teach us any more tricks, old man? Our money suddenly not good enough for you?", Drescher said.

"You don't never pay me with money. You pay me with booze", Lassiter replied. His words were slow and even. He sounded like he was perpetually on the verge of nodding out of consciousness—like he had one foot in and one foot out of the waking world.

Drescher grabbed Lassiter by the back of his neck and shook him like he was trying to rattle the change out of his pockets.

He didn't manage to knock any coins loose, but Drescher's vigorous shaking did manage to uncover a couple of the weird, hieroglyphic-like "prison style" tattoos Lassiter usually kept concealed under several layers of filthy flannel shirts.

"What have we here?", Drescher asked. He grabbed Lassiter by the wrist and yanked his sleeve down, exposing a good sixteen inches of alien looking runes that looked like they were the unholy combination of Asgardian runes, Egyptian hieroglyphics, Norwegian Death Metal band logos, and the last ten covers of Crop Circle Magazine Quarterly.

"I didn't do nothin' to you kids! I did the opposite of nothin', in fact. I taught you's things that nobody oughtta know!" Lassiter howled in his most intimidating voice (which wasn't very). His scarcity of teeth caused him to arbitrarily whistle when he spoke above a whisper. It was painfully embarrassing to witness. Most people were polite enough not to acknowledge it.

The Dark Drivers—and Drescher, in particular— found it uproariously funny. They laughed the kind of deep belly laugh one only laughs when they're half-faking it and intentionally trying to be a huge jerk.

Lassiter reached into the stretched out waste band of his filthy sweatpants and pulled out an intricately ornate dagger that looked older than time itself and at least as long and as wide as a healthy newborn infant.

"Hey now, pal!", Drescher cooed, putting on his friendliest voice, "There's no need for that here. We're friends, man. Just havin' a laugh...".

Drescher's condescension made Lassiter furious.

"Now we're friends", Lassiter sneered. He poked the tip of his blade in Drescher's direction and laughed his own deep belly laugh (made all the more creepy by that weird whistle of his) when the big, self-styled bully flinched in fear. The other members of Drescher's crew joined right in.

And that's when he started to get mad.

"Listen, old man! You want to act tough? I can do that. You clearly don't care about your own well-being (as is evidenced by the fact that you sleep in the gutter in a pile of your own filth—not to mention you testing fate here by pointing that pig-sticker in my direction)...but I've seen a young kid with eyes the exact same shade of green as yours come by from time to time and show you some kindness—droppin' off sandwiches and the like—what if I had a couple of my guys take this matter up with her? You think she's as tough a customer as you are, old man?"

Lassiter just gnashed his teeth and stared at Drescher.

Drescher laughed one of those big, belly laughs again.

"Yeah? What do you think, Old Timer? You like the sound of that?"

Lassiter folded in on himself. His shoulders slumped, his knees bent, and the light went out of his eyes. Drescher's threat had broken him.

In true bully fashion, Drescher took comfort in the object of his ridicule's misery. The old man might know a couple of magic tricks, but that didn't mean he was immune to intimidation.

Drescher swaggered over to Lassiter and grabbed him by the jaw. He raised the sniveling old man's head so that they were eye-to-eye.

"What say we skip all the kid's stuff and move right onto the big league mumbo jumbo?"

Drescher wasn't sure...but he thought he saw the light return to Lassiter's eyes for a moment.

CHAPTER TWO

The pain was excruciating.

Lassiter was using his ornate dagger (an "athame" he called it—whatever that meant) to carve occult symbols into every inch of exposed flesh on Drescher's body. They were the same arcane scribbles Drescher had on his body, only much more plentiful—starting just beneath both of his bottom eyelids and stretching all the way down to the top of his big toes.

It felt like, well...exactly what it sounds like— like having a smelly lunatic use a rusty knife to

21

carve a bunch of mystical gobbledygook into your skin—but Drescher didn't care. A little bit of pain, a gnarly staph infection or two—it didn't matter, so long as the old man delivered on his promise of power. His whole life, all Drescher wanted was to be someone capable, someone strong, someone folks were afraid of.

That's how Drescher viewed the world: there were bullies, and there were the bullied. There were criminals and the criminalized, cops and robbers. The entirety of human history, human existence was all about power—who had it, and who wanted it.

Drescher wanted it. Bad. And if this would help him get it, he'd do it. He'd grit his teeth through the pain if it meant that at the end of it he'd be better, stronger, faster than before. He closed his eyes and imagined he was being tattooed, or pierced, or taking a scalding hot shower—something he decided to do of his own accord, something that was a means to an end, something that gave the pain meaning.

Suddenly, and quickly as he had started, Lassiter stopped.

Drescher slowly opened one eye and peeked at

the old man—half afraid of what he was going to find. What he saw validated that fear: Lassiter's eyes glowed a sickly neon green. His mouth appeared to be packed with dry ice. Little sparks of electricity traveled up and down the lengths of his arms.

"This one is...not *The one*", Lassiter said in a voice that sounded like a vacuum cleaner sucking up a handful of pennies and screws—though, it seemed more like someone was talking through him, rather than him speaking of his own volition. Maybe something.

Maybe it was the blood loss? Maybe he had gone into some kind of shock? Before Drescher could get his bearings together and ascertain fact from fiction Lassiter quickly jerked his head to the right and then leapt through the bathroom window, and went racing off into the desert.

Drescher had never seen a human being move so fast.

CHAPTER THREE

"Cheater!", Flynn's opponent screamed at the top of his lungs as he climbed out of his dragster and lumbered over towards him.

Flynn tried his best to pretend as if he didn't hear the guy. This sort of thing was old hat to him. It happened just about anytime Flynn got behind the wheel—some sore loser (usually some entitled meat head in a cherry off-the-rack ride that somebody assured him was the absolute best car money could buy who just couldn't believe that some poor grease monkey's son in a rusted bucket of scraps he

Frankensteined together from junkyard scraps had the audacity to make him question his investment) always accused him of bending the rules...which was particularly funny, because, at least in the underground circles Flynn raced in, there weren't any to bend.

"Hey, I'm talkin' to you!" the lunkhead shouted again, as if there was a single human being within fifteen miles who hadn't heard him the first time he opened up his big, dumb mouth.

Flynn balled his fists up, but he kept putting one foot in front of the other. He knew that if he stopped walking then the big, loud lug would try to coerce him into fist fighting—and Flynn preferred to settle his scores on the asphalt.

"I said..."

Flynn's new best friend clamped his hand on Flynn's shoulder and spun him around. He caught a glimpse of the guy's car. It wasn't pretty. The tires were practically melted. The axle was all out of whack. Engine coolant was leaking in a manner that, if you squinted real hard, made the car look like it was crying. The vehicle's owner looked like he was about to join in—his eyes were glassy, his forehead was shiny with sweat, he was grinding his teeth so hard Flynn swore he could almost spot sparks.

"I bet you think you're pretty hot stuff right about now..."

"Yep" Flynn said, before pivoting on one foot and forgetting about the comment entirely.

Flynn was a terrible conversationalist. He knew that, and he accepted it.

For a young man so dedicated to personal growth on the race track, his casual acceptance of being less-than-perfect when it came to human interaction was more than a little discordant but he thought of it like this: sharks didn't worry about their inability to do crossword puzzles, Albert Einstein didn't lose sleep over his terrible grooming skills. Being well-rounded is for college applicants and Miss America contestants. Flynn just wanted to burn rubber.

"Hey!"

Flynn spun back around and was genuinely surprised to see his opponent still standing there. but Flynn caught up to speed once the enraged hulk smashed a dirty fist into his jaw.

Flynn hit the ground with a horrible thud—the kind that makes (and did, in fact, make) people turn their heads and ask each other "Did you hear that?".

Flynn hated fighting. He wasn't terrible at it—but even a victory felt like a loss. There was no art to it, no skill. It wasn't like racing, wherein there was always a clear winner and a clear loser. Unless somebody flat out died (which would be horrible), there was no way to tell who won. And even if there was some way to identify a clear "winner"-- what would that even mean? Does the guy with the strongest right hook automatically have the most valid opinion? Not for nothin', but Flynn usually found the exact opposite to be true.

A crowd had gathered around to chant "Fight! Fight!" over and over again, but Flynn—like any rational human being—ignored them. Giving in to peer pressure wasn't Flynn's style. He was more of a leader. He belonged at the head of the pack.

"You got lucky, punk" Flynn's rival said, the adrenaline in is voice making it quiver just enough for Flynn to notice.

Flynn looked the big bully right in the eye, wiped the red from his split lip on the back of his sleeve, and smiled as wide as he could manage.

"Maybe you're right", Flynn said.

The thug crossed his arms and grinned triumphantly.

"Rematch? I'll switch you cars. And I'll drive - - backwards.", Flynn said. Then he tossed him the keys.

...And the crowd grew silent.

CHAPTER FOUR

The teenage racers looked down from atop the gnarliest stretch of road in town: a little patch of land the local teenagers affectionately referred to as "Screaming Skull Suicide Curve". Three guesses as to why.

Seeing his rival behind the wheel of The Big Daddy made Flynn feel a little uneasy (like watching a stranger stretch out the neck on his favorite t-shirt, or spotting some stranger holding hands with an ex-girlfriend).

Flynn wasn't as adept at piloting an automatic

as he was at driving a manual, but that's like saying that Michaelangelo wasn't as good with charcoal as he was with oil paints. If it had a motor and least one wheel, Flynn could make it sing.

"Vroom! Vroom!" the engines roared.

The sound of the two young men's engines were deafening by themselves, but added to the cacophony of the cheers and jeers from the assembled crowd (most of the onlookers from the drag race tagged along for this ride, too...hoping to see another fight. Or maybe even a wipe out. Or possibly both. If racing fans were one thing, it was predictable) they were absolutely senses-shattering.

"Vroom! Vroom!" they roared again.

Flynn glanced over at the other racer. He was chewing on his bottom lip and flexing and unflexing his arms. Clearly on edge. Obviously as nervous and uncomfortable in The Big Daddy as Flynn was in this shiny, store-bought mobile.

Motor sports had that effect on some people. They made the heart race, the brain buzz, the blood boil. They made folks remember they were alive. They granted people who spent the rest of their days trapped in dead end jobs, locked inside cubicles, making zero progress on their personal goals, the illusion of forward momentum. In short: they got average people goin'.

That's how Flynn knew he wasn't normal. For him, moving at a million miles per hour felt normal. It was the other stuff, the sitting still during class, the trying to make polite conversation with other kids, the focus it took to get through a chapter of a book...that's what came hard for him. That's what felt unnatural. That's what made his breath come short and his heart pound like a big kettle drum in his ears.

A ridiculously attractive, dark skinned girl in denim cutoffs and wedges that were about as tall as she was pulled a cherry-red bandanna out of her perfectly coiffed hair and dropped it on to the street, signifying the beginning of the race.

The guys took off.

Flynn laid into his ignition pedal for all it was worth, pushing the machine—and his body—to their limits. His teeth rattled in his skull. His eyeballs shook in their sockets. His stomach felt like it was doing somersaults. But the dumbfounded look on his opponent's face as he zipped by in his own ride made it all worthwhile.

Doing the impossible was what Flynn was best at—and not by cheating, or by throwing ridiculous amounts of money at people to do all the hard work of fine tuning an automobile for him. Flynn liked to think that he got where he was going because of his dedication to the craft, his practice and hard work... but he sometimes he felt the undeniable presence of some other invisible, intangible factor at work as well.

Flynn didn't believe in fate (the idea of sitting in the passenger's seat when it came to racing towards his destiny made his skin crawl), but how else could one explain the fact that he always seemed to have just enough gas to make it across the finish line, exactly the right amount of tread left on his tires to pull off a death-defying turn, that his vehicles always went precisely as fast as he needed them to—even if that speed defied what mathematics said should by physically possible.

He knew that it sounded a little arrogant, that it

was something he could never say aloud without being ridiculed, but he felt like he was born to drive—and that every vehicle on earth was made to be driven by him.

Case in point: Flynn was starting to hit his stride. It took him a second to acclimate to his enemy's ride but he was there.

The problem that most people had when they dealt with automobiles is that they treated it like nothing more than a tool, some necessary evil between them and their goal. They never consider that the machines might have their own needs, their own (for lack of a better word) will.

Flynn heard that will in the sputter of an engine. He felt it in the sudden tug of an axle. Machines spoke to him, and he listened. And he responded accordingly. He took care of his machines, and they, in turn, took care of him.

...Which is why it physically hurt Flynn to look in his rear view mirror and catch a glimpse of some idiot stumbling right out in front of him onto the asphalt...

CHAPTER FIVE

Flynn recited a string of bad words and swerved off the road. He burned with a desire to win—but not at the cost of a human life.

He knew that should probably get out of the car and make sure that old fool was okay, but Flynn was afraid that if he stepped foot outside he'd probably go into a berserker rage and strangle the clumsy idiot for making him forfeit the race...and that would defeat the point of swerving out of the way in the first place.

So Flynn sat in the car, banging his head on the steering wheel. Waiting for his anger to subside.

After a couple of minutes Flynn looked up. His opponent wasn't the best racer in the world, but surely his opponent had pushed The Big Daddy across the finish line by now, right?

Flynn squinted, and saw that he had—but that the same bum who had run him off the road was now assaulting that guy too, jumping up and down on the hood of The Big Daddy and shouting incomprehensible nonsense.

Flynn bolted out of the car and stomped towards The Big Daddy. As he got closer he started to pick up a little bit of the old man's rambling...

"You're not The One! Your car smells like him, it's got The One's aura all over it! He poured his heart soul into this thing. It's drenched in intent, fortified by the will of The One who was born to race between realities! This is his chariot, his stead, his sacred totem

Flynn's rival puffed his chest out at the raving madman.

"Yeah, well I don't know who you think you are, but you're certainly nothing special either, dirt bag," the big lug yelled.

The old man made a weird shape with his fist and then promptly drove it into the insulting young man's throat.

The big lug fell to his knees, clutching his throat and gasping for air.

Flynn and the homeless man both just stood there a while, watching and listening to the guy make angry little drowning sounds until what sounded like a swarm of thousands of enraged insects broke their concentration.

Flynn tore his eyes off the ridiculous scene playing out in front of him and looked over his shoulder. He quickly discerned the source of the infernal buzzing: about a dozen motorcycles (Vintage, American models—no plastic, neon, foreign toys in sight) rolling over the horizon. They spewed long trails of thick, black smog into the air behind them, tainting the air around them with their very presence.

"Ummm..." Flynn managed to mumble, surprised he had the mental fortitude to say anything at all.

It wasn't that Flynn was scared—the sight of anything with an engine in it could never illicit any feeling in his heart other than appreciation—it was that he had no context in which to place this sort of thing. Within the space of an hour he had been in two races, gotten socked in the jaw, and witnessed the big jerk who'd been hounding him be taken down by a skinny old homeless man.

No, Flynn didn't scare easily...but he did, on occasion, worry. And a dozen loud, dirty bikers looking for trouble was bound to make just about anyone's knees rattle...especially when he realized that his car was stuck in a ditch, and he had no means by which to get the Heck out of dodge.

"I told those noisy boogers I wouldn't let 'em have it!", the insane old man yelled, "They think they want what's in my brain meats! But they don't! Nobody in they right mind would want anything to do with what's hiding in thereabouts!"

Flynn's recently-throat-punched rival, clearly having had enough craziness for one day, took off running in the opposite direction.

Flynn sincerely contemplated joining him. Shockingly enough, nothing quite like this had ever happened in Flynn's short dozen-and-some-change years on the planet and he had absolutely no idea what do do.

"What do they want with you?", Flynn shouted at the old coot.. "And while we're askin' questions: what in the Heck is goin' on here?".

"I'll tell you...but you've got to keep up!" Lassiter said, before running off into the forest.

Flynn obliged the old coot. He was never one to turn down a race.

CHAPTER SIX

Lassiter was startled by the young man running alongside —and not because of the questions he asked, or because of the clearly annoyed timber of his voice, but because his soul radiated such brilliant white light that looking directly at him made the liquid swirling around his eyeballs start to boil.

If you had caught him yesterday, Lassiter would have told you that he did have a screw loose. He would have echoed the sentiments of nice mister Doctor Benton down at the free clinic and told you that the chemicals in his brain were all screwed up—that it wasn't his fault, that it didn't make him a bad person or make The Good Lord love him any less—but that he was born irreparably broken... missing some vital element in his genetic makeup that would've kept him whole, and clean, and blind to the mythical horrors that normal people are decent enough to have no inkling of.

But that was before tonight, before that long haired, short tempered motorcycle thug convinced him (more like forced him, under threat of physical harm) that he should work his arcane arts on the big galoot.

After years and years of suppressing that side of himself, of actively denying the very existence of magick at all, it felt odd falling back into the habit. Lassiter, unsure at first as to whether or not he still had enough mojo to pull anything serious off, was shocked at how easy it was to get back into the swing of the old ways. The familiar "click" in his head as he shifted his perception away from the quotidian and into the realms ethereal, the accompanying voices that always manifested during the transition, the weird shadows that formed in the corners of his eyes that he was never quick enough to catch a decent glance of—they were all exactly where he had left them.

And even though Lassiter was humbled in the presence of those cosmic forces for whom he lacked the proper words to encapsulate, the fact that he had access to an aspect of the world kept out of the reach of most filled Lassiter him with a malicious pride that he was all too happy to take out on his would-be-tormentor, Drescher.

He wanted agency in the realms eternal? He wanted to make himself visible to the monstrous tyrant-gods who had nothing but disdain for the mortal realm, and all who called it a home? Fine.

Lassiter, at Drescher's request, cast upon him the most powerful incantation in his grim repertoire: The Rite of The Road Rager.

That name, "The Road Rager" was his translation—but it was just as good as any other. The being had gone by many names since man first became aware of his existence and tried (in vain) to encapsulate all that he was in their petty language (a vulgar series of wet clicks and whistles that could never hope to accurately represent even a fraction of The Truth). The Greeks called him "Hermes", and told tales about him racing from the top of Mount Olympus (the highest point in existence) to the mortal realm in the blink of a mortal's eye. The Nordic people knew him as the Holy mechanic "Zoran", the legendary inventor of machines of impossible speeds, and creator of the legendary hero Thor's "War Chariot". The Hare Krishnas referred to him as the demigod Surya, who piloted a faster-than-thought, solar powered UFO across the morning sky.

...Which was why Lassiter was such an idiot for calling their attention to him, and our world, again.

For decades Lassiter had kept to the straight and narrow, forsaking the easy route of magick for the slow, trudging, unglamorous laws of physics. In his heyday he was a street sorcerer of great renown. His name was feared by devils and angels alike. Magicians, exorcists, conjurers and wise men all spoke of his exploits as if they were the legendary trials of some forgotten hero from a long forgotten mythology. He was a celebrity in the occult underground, an astronaut, pushing the boundaries of what was thought possible.

...Until those boundaries pushed back.

The act that pushed Lassiter over the edge was a fouled up invocation of the being he came to call "The Road Rager". He—through great expense to both his bank account and his sanity—had come into the possession of the true name of The Road Rager (he couldn't pronounce it for the life of him, but it was written down—in what language, Lassiter would never know—on six scrolls of indeterminate origin, in the blood of a creature that didn't exist, put up for sale on the internet by the clueless relatives of a suburban mage in Miskatonic County, Massachusetts who was institutionalized after delving too deep in his own investigation of The Elder Gods), and proceeded to carve the lion's share of the glyphs into his flesh, in a foolish attempt to get his attention, and siphon off just a fraction of his incredible power.

It worked. And when The Road Rager cast his eye on Lassiter he experienced an existential crisis that would've made Noah himself quake with fear.

Lassiter saw things that were never meant to be seen by a mortal man. Lassiter, considered himself to be a pioneer in all things obscure, was exposed to concepts so macabre they shattered his sense of reality.

When he finally "recovered" it was a decade later and he had gone from being one of the most revered occultists of his day to being an acrid smelling public nuisance who was regularly pelted with rocks by the local neighborhood teenagers. He had been touched by the god of speed, and all that had happened was that his life was fast forwarded directly into the toilet.

Lassiter swore that he'd never repeat the ritual. He had only completed a fourth of the ceremony during his initial attempt and still the effects were potent enough to have changed the course of his entire life. And certainly not for the better.

But Drescher had forced his hand. He threatened the one thing in all of the world(s) that Lassiter cared about at all: Krystal. His niece, his strength, his lifeline.

Lassiter had reached a point in his life when very

little made him angry. Watching the fortunate waste food and money, waking up to the smell of gasoline and a gang of bored teenagers looming over him with a book of matches and the look of mischief in their eyes, these things irked him. But someone insulting—no, worse than that—insinuating violence towards the one human in all of the world who still treated him with the dignity he deserved (not just as the most accomplished magic user since King Solomon, but as a man), that made him very, truly angry.

And it was in that anger that Lassiter agreed to cast the very same spell on Drescher, a curse disguised as a blessing.

Lassiter had hoped that the spell would have blown Drescher's mind, that the sudden influx of power and perspective would've fried his circuits as hard as it had Lassiter's so long ago...but Drescher didn't blink. He didn't beg Lassiter to stop. All he said was "more".

So the thing that was once called Hermes, Zoran, Surya, The Road Rager didn't like being bound so intimately to an unworthy vessel, one so unwashed of flesh and impure of heart—so it did what any self-respecting, power tripping deity would—it cursed Drescher for his hubris.

The only problem was...Drescher didn't mind.

CHAPTER SEVEN

Flynn tossed the old man over his shoulder before he had a chance to answer (and, really, even if he did answer—what were the odds of anything he said making rational sense anyway?) and took off running.

Flynn ran, pumping his legs as fast as he could manage with an old man on his back, but The Dark Drivers kept on his trail with a preternatural doggedness that was, frankly, terrifying. A couple times Flynn had thought that he'd thrown them off, only to witness one of the riders tilt their head back and sniff the air for a moment before perfectly correcting their course. It had to have been for show—nothing more than an intimidation tactic—but it worked.

Suddenly one of the motorcycle-bound henchmen raced close, driving his street bike NOT on the street and right at them, Flynn committed an act of utmost desperation: he threw the rag-doll-like body of the man he was attempting to save directly at the biker (hoping against hope that the old drunk was limp enough to avoid any lasting damage). The guy never saw it coming.

Flynn managed to take hold of the bike before it crushed the both of them. He grabbed Lassiter's wrist and kicked the borrowed bike into high gear, letting the forward propulsion of the vehicle wrench the old man free from the tangle of grunts and broken bones the fallen biker had become.

Lassiter trailed behind Flynn's bike for a minute, soaring in the air like a superhero or some sort of weird, bearded, garbage-smelling kite before Flynn yanked him down onto the back of the bike. Lassiter clung to the seat for dear life, facing the opposite direction of Finn.

"You drive! I'll play the lookout!" Lassiter slurred, clearly unfazed by being used as a human bowling ball.

Flynn didn't even bother to answer him. He kept his mind on the prize: keeping them both out of the clutches of their pursuers.

He didn't know who this mysterious elderly stranger was, but Flynn knew that the jerks who disrupted his race wanted to hurt him, and that was reason enough to play keep-away with the guy.

Flynn watched in horror as the leader of the gang (or, at least Finn assumed he was the head honcho from the gruesome tribal markings on the man's face, and the way the others fell in line behind him as they rode) sped right over the body of his fallen comrade on his way to get to Flynn.

This clearly wasn't just a race to these people. It was life and death. And it was more than young Flynn Friedrich had accounted for.

CHAPTER EIGHT

Flynn almost didn't hear the police sirens over the sound of his throbbing heartbeat, threatening to burst through his chest. Two police cruisers were coming right towards them

The sound of police wasn't usually something that a young drag racer welcomed, but this time was different. Flynn knew that he was in over his head. All this carnage, this violence...it was too much.

Flynn swerved hard and made a u-turn. He revved the bike into high gear, rocketing towards the police cars at such high speed one of Lassiter's remaining teeth shook loose.

"What are you doing? Playing chicken with the fuzz?" Lassiter howled, clutching onto the motorcycle for dear life.

"Handing you over to the cops", Flynn said. "I don't know what you've gotten me mixed up in— and let's be clear, I don't really want to know—but I don't want any part of it. This kind of thing...it's not what I do. It's not who I am".

"So, it's not what you've done, and it's not who you've been. Who cares? You live as long as I have, you start to understand that identity is one of the most fragile things there is."

Flynn bit his lip. They were moments away from splattering onto the hood of a cop car.

"That's how you're gonna play it, huh? That right, cowards?" Drescher roared over the sound of both his and Flynn's engines. Thick black smoke trickled out of the sides of his mouth as he spoke.

Flynn blinked hard, trying to convince himself that the adrenaline in his bloodstream was causing him to hallucinate Drescher's monstrous qualities.

Drescher held one hand high and squeezed off

a couple of gestures to his crew. Moving as one, they fell in line and drove off in unison towards the rising moon.

Flynn swerved from hitting the police cruisers at the last second and exhaled a heavy sigh of relief. His allayment was short-lived, however.

"You two off the bike and on the ground!" as four armed officers shouted, running towards Flynn and Lassiter with their weapons drawn.

"Umm...I surrender?" Flynn said

CHAPTER NINE

"Lightweight" Lassiter laughed from his corner of the cell. "Ain't you ever been chased by a gang of ghouls on motorbikes before?"

"Ghouls?" Flynn asked.

"Yeah, 'ghouls'. What, yer parents don't let you leave the house or somethin'?" Lassiter asked, annoyed.

"At least I have a house" Flynn replied. He wasn't usually this snarky, but recent circumstances (namely—almost being lynched by horrifying monster-bikers and then getting locked up in prison with and taunted by the curmudgeonly old bum who got him in this whole predicament in the first place) had him a little on edge.

"Not anymore you don't. You just drove headfirst towards a fleet of police vehicles on a stolen motorcycle belonging to a dead gang member. And you're hangin' out with me. Plus, if you do try to plead innocent, your only alibi is that you were illegally drag racing with a bunch of jokers who'll never corroborate your story, 'cause it'll implicate them".

Lassiter laughed for a good thirteen minutes, choking and wheezing for air.

And then the duo heard the low rumble of about a dozen motorcycle engines approaching, from off in the distance.

Lassiter stopped laughing.

Their engines were so loud they rattled the bars of Flynn and Lassiter's prison cell.

"Geez, those guys are persistent. What do they want with you, anyway?" Flynn asked Lassiter.

Lassiter looked off into the distance.

"You're lucky. You're so young...if you find

yourself unlucky enough to live as long as I have, you'll find there's a whole road of mistakes between your age and mine" Lassiter said, his voice full of remorse.

"We'll see" Flynn replied.

"Now from the sound of things," Lassiter said, sadly, "sounds like our friends are closing in. It's a shame, too. Once they rend the flesh from your bones and devour your soul whole there'll be nothing on Earth that'll be able to stop them".

Flynn stomped across the room and grabbed Lassiter by his collar.

"This isn't some game to me, alright? It's my life! Here I am, worrying about what my dad's going to say when he comes to pick me up, freaking out about whether or not I'm going to have my license suspended and you're telling me that what I should be concerned with is being eaten alive by a bunch of cannibalistic, biker-jerks? What's happening here, man? Who are these people? Who are you?

CHAPTER TEN

Drescher kicked the door to the police station down like it was nothing at all. He was fearless back when he was mortal ("What do I gotta fear", he used to say, "I got nothin' to lose"), and now that he was...not mortal...he was even more obnoxious.

"Knock! Knock! Anybody home...?" Drescher shouted with a booming voice ten times louder than his shriveled up lungs should have been capable of managing.

The police station was less than impressive. Like everything in town, it was small, obsolete, and ineffectual—more a simulacrum of an actual police station than a real, functioning law enforcement structure. It was manned by two guys who did their best—a couple of "good old boys" who enjoyed the local notoriety their uniforms afforded, but hadn't quite earned their titles.

"Whuh-whu-what seems to be the trouble, sir?" One of the officers said, slowly walking towards Drescher (and his gang, who began filing in through the door behind him). "Can I help you, son?".

Drescher grabbed the man by his throat and lifted him several inches off of the ground. He pulled the officer of the law's face close to his and inhaled deeply. A thick, green smog emanated from the man's nostrils and open, screaming mouth and flowed into Drescher's. It seemed to have a restorative effect of Drescher, smoothing out his unseemly wrinkles and inflating his chest ever so slightly, correcting the exhausted slouch he had walked in with.

The exchange had the opposite effect on the police officer. Flynn watched in absolute horror as the man withered before his eyes. He seemed to crumple from the inside out, to age within seconds.

"Ghouls sometimes feed on the life force of the living" Lassiter whispered in Flynn's ear. "Think of 'em like 'energy vampires', if that makes any sense..."

For the first time since being locked up Flynn was grateful to be behind thick, steel bars.

"And those bars aren't going to do squat. Sorry".

"Are they, uh...are they dead?" Flynn asked, as he watched Drescher and his goons pounce on the remaining prison guard and give him the same, gruesome soul-sucking treatment they gave his partner.

"Nope. The Ghouls' got no use for dead folks. They establish a connection with their victims, make living mummies out 'em. As long as they're kept breathin' they keep pumping life force energy into the ghoul that messed 'em up in the first place. They're like long-range batteries made out of meat."

Flynn gagged a little at Lassiter's description. The guy had a way with words. That's for sure. If only he was as proficient with a bar of soap...

"Did you make all of them like that?" Flynn tried

not to let his voice betray his anger. But it did.

"Just the big one" Lassiter answered quietly, not bothering to mask his self-hatred with his usual trademark aloofness. "He must've made the rest himself. They won't be nearly as strong"

Flynn took a good look at Drescher's flunkies. They were weird, misshapen parodies of their leader. The runes Drescher carved into them certainly had a transformative affect (their gums had receded—giving the appearance of fangs, the skin had started to rot from their fingers—giving way to sharpened bone claws).

Drescher and his posse sniffed the air. They caught Flynn's and Lasiter's scent (which, to be honest, wasn't that hard even if one wasn't fully equipped with supernatural senses), and started shuffling down the hall towards the both of them.

"You sure about that, man?" Flynn gulped.

"I'm not sure of a whole lot these days..." Lassiter answered.

Flynn heard a slight quiver in the man's voice that he wished he hadn't.

CHAPTER ELEVEN

Drescher's monstrous thugs ripped Flynn's and his cell door off its hinges with less effort than some people use to pop open a bag of potato chips.

Drescher stepped inside the cramped prison cell and looked Flynn dead-in-the-eye. "I'm gonna gut you and anyone you care about for slowing me down tonight."

"Lucky for you I'm the only one you have to worry about." Flynn bluffed.

Just then, a panicked a figure rushed in through the hole in the wall that was formerly the door to the police station.

"Flynn? Flynn" The man shouted.

Flynn shouted "No! What are you even doing here?"

Drescher lunged, a creepy smile spreading across his awful countenance. He pounced on the man like some sort of diseased jungle cat—like a leopard with leprosy—and grabbed him by the back of his head. He pulled the poor, confused man's face towards his and inhaled greedily, gulping down mouthfuls of the man's soul.

"Get your dirty hands off my father!" Flynn screamed, lunging towards Drescher for all he was worth.

One of Drescher's minions instinctively dove in the way of Flynn as he moved towards his leader. The big, creepy abomination threw its arms around Flynn and held him like a vice grip, forcing him to watch helplessly as his father had everything that made him, him sucked down by a demon in a leather jacket.

"You gonna cry, youngblood?" Drescher laughed, in between swallows.

Flynn stomped hard on his captor's big toe, causing the monster to let go of Flynn and ball his hands up into punchin' fists.

Flynn used the close quarters to his advantage, ducking under the minion's first swing and vaulting across the room to where Drescher was tormenting his dad. He struck out at Drescher wildly, swinging his arms like windmill propellers.

Drescher swatted Flynn across the face and sent him soaring towards the back wall of the prison.

Flynn thought the crunching sound of his own cartilage folding in on itself was nausea-inducing but then was momentarily relieved as he felt nothing and his world went suddenly black.

CHAPTER TWELVE

Lassiter was well aware that he was older than dirt. He knew full well that his muscles were too old to be of any real use. But he was a magician, and magicians dealt in symbols. And if he was going to die, then at least he would end his time on earth looking like he wasn't a total coward...even if he lived the lion's share of his life as such.

The old man launched himself at Drescher, fist first.

Drescher blocked it and leaned in and attempted to absorb Lassiter's energy. He hadn't accounted on all of the horrific visions that came along with that.

Drescher recoiled. He howled with rage and spit on the floor, trying to get the taste out of his mouth—but that's just it—the "taste" wasn't in his mouth at all. It was lodged in the very core of who he was (his "soul" if you believed in that kind of stuff)—stuck like a splinter in too deep to dig out.

Lassiter's body hit the cement with a nasty thud. His eyes were dark and his breathing was shallow... but the grin plastered onto his face was larger than any Drescher had ever seen in his entire life.

Drescher stumbled, clutching his head in pain and no longer wanting any more of what Lassiter had to offer. The old man and the kid were gonna die here in a few minutes anyhow from their injuries. "What are you idiots gawking at?" Drescher taunted them. "Let's ride!"

Without saying a word they all knew exactly which direction in which to head. It was like the information was encoded into their horrible new nervous systems and they all headed off into the darkness leaving behind only death.

CHAPTER THIRTEEN

"What a stupid way to die..." Flynn said, weakly, and to no one in particular as he awoke from blissful unconsciousness.

The police station looked like a tornado had blown through, and then set the place on fire as it left.

"Seen a lot of people die in my time, son. In a lot of different ways. Not a one of 'em looked anything close to 'smart'..." Lassiter answered, scaring Flynn half to death.

"Holy crud!" Flynn yelled, half terrified that the

old man was still kicking, and half grateful.

Flynn was having trouble making his legs listen to his brain, but his arms still had enough juice left in them to crawl his way over to Lassiter.

"How are you even still breathing?" Flynn gasped. He worried that he used up the last of his strength to do so. The pain was incredible.

"I may be old, but I'm not all dried out yet. I've still got a trick or two up my sleeve" Lassiter wheezed through his broken smile a smile that looked like it belonged more on a cracked fun house mirror than a human being.

Flynn glanced over at his father and immediately wished he hadn't. Mr. Friedrich didn't have the good fortune of having some vague mystical powers on his side, protecting him from harm. All he had was an ungrateful son who stayed out too late, drove too fast, and didn't call home often enough—without whom none of this would have happened.

Despite the pain, Flynn raged with anger. Flynn knew he was dying as his injuries were severe. He knew his father was now bound to a ruthless killer and he knew that all of this was mostly his own fault.

"You got anything up your sleeve that I can use to help my dad?" Flynn gasped.

Lassiter's smile faded.

"Can't say that I do, kid. Even I'm not that good..." Lassiter answered.

"...Then how about something that I can use to avenge him?"

Lassiter's smile returned, "That I can do...but you ain't gonna like it."

CHAPTER FOURTEEN

The next thing Flynn knew he was propped up on the toilet in the police officers' bathroom, covered in bandages and having water splashed onto his face by...no...it couldn't be...by Krystal—that impossibly pretty and even more impossibly mean girl from school.

"What are you doing here?" Flynn tried to say, but all that came out was a stream of unintelligible mumbles. His mouth was too dry and his cheeks were too swollen to form real, actual human words.

"Shush. Don't try to talk," Krystal said, handing

Flynn a small paper cup full of water, "you've been through a lot. I think your body's going into shock".

Flynn gulped it down. He tried to stand, but his legs were still shaking from being pumped full of adrenaline.

"I don't have time to go into shock! I've got to get out there and stop the savages who did this to my father before--"

Krystal bit her lip and looked down at the floor. She idly played with the roll of gauze she held in her hands.

"I'm sorry. I didn't know one of those guys out here used to be...er, is your dad..."

"Thanks," Flynn said as he got up and made his way for the door, "but I have to get rolling".

"Hey! Slow down!" Krystal shouted as she chased after him.

Flynn fells to his knees, involuntarily shaking from the pain and shock. He searched his mind for an answer as to how he wound up this way. He felt his memories unfolding like a lotus, peeling back layers of self, giving him way more information than he asked it for. He saw what had happened to him—Lassiter used up the last of his life-force marking Flynn's skin with the same mystical sigils that covered his—but Flynn also caught glimpses of other memories inside his own head which couldn't possibly have belonged to him: visions of cowboys driving unfathomably powerful steeds across the open plains, Kahunas surfing down waves of molten lava on Tiki head surfboards that refused to burn, superhuman conductors who drove steam engines whose engines were powered by magical emeralds instead of coal...

"Your markings--" Krystal said, her voice bringing Flynn back to planet Earth, "they look just like my Uncle Laz's. Did you guys know each other before this? Is that why you were here together tonight? Is that why...?"

"Wait—you know that old coot? How are the two of you acquainted?" Flynn interrupted. Having never before used the word "acquainted" in a sentence he prayed that he had pronounced it properly, and not come off like a total goon. It bothered him immensely to realize that his head was filled with the names of hundreds of options, from dozens of different pantheons, for gods to which he could offer prayer.

"He's was...is...literally my uncle", She replied, eying Flynn nervously. "'Uncle Laz'". "So, you're the one who brought him sandwiches?" Flynn said, grasping for memories of anecdotes Lassiter had shared in the brief but ridiculously impactful time their lives had intersected.

A brief moment of hope flashed behind the girl's eyes for just a quick second (before she consciously choked it down).

"He talked about me?" She asked, straining to keep her voice nice and even.

"Told me everything about you except for your name" Flynn replied, extending his hand in her direction, "Small world, huh?'.

She took one look at Flynn's bloody, rune-bearing mitt and shot him a glance that seemed to say "do you really expect me touch that thing". Flynn didn't notice. Something about spending a whole day drag racing, bickering with street wizards, being transformed into a scarred, supernatural warrior and then doing battle with a gang of soul-eating biker demons had done serious damage to the portion of his brain that recognized subtlety. He kept his hand out there.

"Don't leave me hangin'" Flynn said, awkwardly.

"We should probably get some more gauze for the road," the girl said as she disappeared into the police station bathroom and began searching for a first aid kit, "you're making a mess all over the place".

Flynn cursed himself (and found that he was equipped with a few more of those than he used to be, too) for acting like such a buffoon. Being a solitary-type-guy he had the privilege of deluding himself into thinking that the reason he didn't often speak with women was because he was "too fast for love"...but now that he was face-to-face with a real, live female specimen he was confronted by the harsh reality that it was probably more due to the fact that he just wasn't any good at it.

"Here, let me help you with that. You keep walking around with those open flesh-carvings exposed like that and you're liable to catch gangrene" she said, emerging with a tiny, white plastic box with a big red cross on the front full of gauze, Isopropyl alcohol, cotton balls, and chewable Aspirin.

She poured a little bit of the rubbing alcohol onto a cotton ball and approached Flynn with a matronly concern that at once terrified and titillated the exhausted, beaten, bleeding teenager.

"I got it..." Flynn said, reaching out and taking the moist bit of white fluff from her before she could apply it to his wounds. Their hands touched. A static shock zapped the both of them. The cotton ball was dropped. They both withdrew their hands and laughed nervously.

"It's fine, really" she said, looking Flynn right in the eye.

"Well, Krystal...You've got a pretty solid handle on the state of things, all things considered" Flynn said, his eyes drifting towards Lassiter's body.

Krystal's eyes followed Flynn's.

"He's still breathing. There's still hope. " Krystal said.

"I don't want to freak you out or anything—but we've got a lot more than hope on our side" Flynn said, before willing two gigantic energy ghost-swords out of the palms of his hands.

"No kidding" Krystal shouted over the sound of the approaching sirens, gesturing towards a couple of duffel bags full of weapons, gadgets and armor she had helped herself to from the armory

The unlikely pair outfitted themselves with Krystal's "borrowed" police gear until the ambulances were practically in the same room as them, and then left the comatose inhabitants of the police station in the care of the emergency medical technicians—people whose job it was to heal others.

Flynn and Krystal had their own mission. And it certainly wasn't to heal anybody...

CHAPTER FIFTEEN

"OK, my car should just be up ahead. Also,this is like, hands down, the weirdest Wednesday I've ever had" Flynn said, mostly to himself.

"For real, though. For really real. Seriously" Krystal echoed.

It was about to get even weirder.

Flynn jumped out of Crystal's mini-van and ran up to The Big Daddy and was devastated to see that getting it out of the ditch tonight was a definite impossibility.

When Flynn touched his faithful gas-powered

companion something odd happened to them both. A switch of sorts clicked on in the back of his head, causing him to recall all of the vehicles he'd driven throughout his immortal career as the earthly instrument of The Road Rager: powerful steeds, devastating man-made contraptions—all equally revered, each of them more an extension of himself than a separate functioning entity. More familiars than vehicles.

The Big Daddy was no exception. And when Flynn hugged the car it seemed to somehow "remember" that legacy, and rise to the challenge it presented. The car seemed to stand up straighter, correcting its own bent chassis and would-be-costly alignment problems. A supernatural force from within seemed to radiate throughout the car, smoothing out dings and dents, regenerating paint over scratches, and pulling air into its tires from Lord only knows where.

"Whoa" Krystal said, admiring the new and improved Bid Daddy.

"Big Daddy, meet Krystal. Krystal, meet The Big Daddy. No offense but we're following them in this." Flynn said, chock full of paternal pride. He leaned in close to Krystal's ear.

"Let's go beat the tar out of some bad guys..."

CHAPTER SIXTEEN

Flynn reached for the key and as he did so the engine roared like something not of this world. When Flynn put his pedal to the metal it accelerated at a velocity so ferocious he feared that his reflexes wouldn't be able to keep up.

Flynn had little to fear as they raced off into the night. Lassiter had somehow managed to channel most of the power of the Road Rager into Flynn but Flynn was also aware something in his mind was blocking the full deluge of ancient and arcane information. Flynn was aware the information was provided to him as needed. It wasn't the constant barrage of information like Lassiter experiences. Lassiter had learned from his own folly and used that information to protect Flynn's sanity.

More so, if Flynn was an excellent driver before his transformation, then now Flynn was— quite simply— a manifestation of speed itself. He anticipated the actions of other drivers with an expertise that boarded on precognition. His could feel the terrain under his tires as easily as if it were underfoot.

In short: he was really, really good.

"Where are we going?" Krystal managed to shout over the sound of metal and rubber defying the laws of physics—and every traffic law in the state of Arizona.

"I don't know," Flynn answered cooly, "it's like I can see their path."

"Then hurry it up!" Krystal replied, trying to mask her fear with bravado.

Flynn grinned.

"If you insist..."

And with that the sound of thunder erupted through the pines.

CHAPTER SEVENTEEN

The Big Daddy flew down Route 66 so fast Krystal swore she saw a roadrunner have a heart attack at the sight of it.

Further down the road, Big Daddy eventually stopped at the sight of four lumbering ghouls who had set up their motorcycles as a makeshift barricade in the center of the street. They brandished axes, chains and weapons they'd picked up along the way.

Flynn unbuckled his seat belt and got out of the car. Krystal tried to follow his lead but Flynn made some complicated gesture with his wrist and caused the doors to lock and her seat belt to tighten of their own accord.

"I've got these ones. You can take the next" he said, and then ignited those two energy ghost-swords he first manifested in front of Krystal, back at the station.

It was like the weapons had a mind of their own:

The one in his right hand screamed out for justice, and Flynn had no interest in standing in its way. He slashed and stabbed with the fury—and the skill—of an ancient samurai, tapping into the skill set of one of the other racers who were gifted with the energy of The Road Rager throughout its legacy.

The blade in his left hand seemed to exist solely to protect the innocent. It leaped into the way whenever Flynn came close to taking a hit from one of the ghoul's swipes, parrying any blows that came its way and creating openings for its companion weapon to get in there and do its thing.

Flynn "remembered" using these sacred tools in other manifestations, in other lives (they weren't always machetes, as they appeared now—sometimes they were katanas, escrima sticks, even sidearms—

whatever was necessary and appropriate for the era in which they were summoned. But always one weapon for protection and one for...justice).

Krystal didn't consider herself a very squeamish person—quite the opposite, actually—but she couldn't bring herself to watch Flynn throw down. The precision with which he incapacitated his enemies was so discordant with how she viewed him (as some nervous, bumbling weirdo she occasionally teased at school) that it actually kind of hurt her brain to see him like this...like a bonafide superhero.

The windows rolled down, the doors clicked unlocked, and Flynn leaned in and said "You cool?"

Krystal just about jumped out of her skin.

"That was...it was...well, it was fast".

Flynn winked at her as he climbed back into The Big Daddy.

"Yeah, well—that's kind of my thing now, isn't it? And to be honest they weren't very good. The rest won't be so easy...especially Drescher."

Krystal blushed.

"Alright, Flynn—what's the plan?" she asked.

Flynn said over the music, "Same as before, we follow them and when we find them, we smite them."

Krystal cranked the radio up and said, "Let's rock!"

CHAPTER EIGHTEEN

Drescher and The Dark Drivers had been traveling down Route 66 for a couple hours, running any motorists who got in their way right off the road...or worse.

These powers that the old man cursed him with were pretty cool, but they came with a lot of baggage, too—not the least of which were these weird, half-forgotten, inherited memories about "The River Nile", and "Planetary Lay Lines", and "convergences of mystical energy". Drescher couldn't spell half of those words, let alone tell you what they meant—but, from putting together bits and pieces of things he had picked up here and there he had mentally assembled what he was fairly confident was the gist of it: that magical energy flowed through the Earth a lot like water, and that there were certain currents that it tended to flow towards—just like water collecting in a stream.

Route 66 was one apparently one of those stream thinamabobs, 'cause Drescher and his gang were drawn to it the way birds were summoned south in the winter. It was beyond compulsion—like something inside of them had to take them in this direction, or it'd wither and die.

Under normal circumstances The Dark Drivers' bikes never would have withstood the rigors of long-term highway travel (they, for the most part, lacked the discipline necessary to become a truly skilled mechanic, like Flynn was. That took actual hard work. They, instead, preferred to just steal new bikes whenever they ran their old ones into the ground)--but, lucky for the Dark Drivers, these weren't normal circumstances. The drivers' mutation seemed to be contagious. They had noticed that the longer they rode their motorcycles, the harder it was to distinguish themselves from their machines. It was if they were beginning to exhale exhaust and they could feel gasoline mixing with the blood in their veins.

But they rode on—partially due to the supernatural drive they felt to do so, but also due in no small part to a macabre fascination they had developed with the process itself. None of the members of The Dark Drivers had any delusions about living forever (gang members rarely do). Dying in a spectacular fashion was pretty much the only way they could guarantee that they'd be remembered at all.

The Dark Drivers had no idea what their pre-programmed destination was. It didn't matter. They knew exactly how they were getting' there.

Suddenly, another compulsion came over Drescher. He clicked on the radio and signaled for his cronies to quiet their engines.

The signal strained to come through on the Dark Drivers' weird, malformed machines, but bits and pieces still managed to find their way to the speakers:

"The Los Angeles Museum Of Natural

History....'The Patron Saints of Speed Exhibition'...
Bzzzzt...you gotta go, go go!"

It was an awkward overlap of a commercial
and the hook from some terrible Top Forty pop
song—but Drescher knew, in his bones, that the bad
reception wasn't a coincidence.

CHAPTER NINETEEN

A wave of Déjà vu washed over Drescher as he and his boys pulled up to The Los Angeles Museum of Natural History—which was odd, seeing as he had never purposefully set foot in a museum in his entire life.

Somehow the décor outside (stories-tall vinyl banners depicting samples of some of the featured "Patron Saints of Speed" exhibition the radio wouldn't shut up about) made him feel at home. And, also...hungry? Was that right?

Drescher figured that he and the rest of the Dark

Drivers were way beyond the needs of the material flesh now. They drove the whole way here from Arizona without stopping once for water, washroom breaks, or rest of any kind.

But, for some reason, looking at a picture of mummified corpse made him sick with hunger. From the rumble of The Dark Drivers' bellies, it sounded like it had the same effect on them.

Suddenly it dawned on Drescher: That crazy old bum's magic! The "saints of speed" theme! The undeniable drive to get here! The reason his transformation wasn't nearly as gross and painful-looking as that of his comrades—it was destiny!

Here he had gone, his entire life, believing that he was just some piece of human refuse, some remainder in the math of infinity...but he had a destiny all the while!

He was supposed to absorb the residual power from those fossilized old bags of bones (he hoped that it'd be as easy it was with the living—like with Lasssiter and Flynn's old man—but he'd grind them down into a protein shake and gulp them right down, if that was what it took) and take his rightful place as the modern god of everything that moved with a quickness.

Yeah. That was it. Drescher could see it now: he'd raise an army a hundred thousand times larger than the one he had now—machine like gangsters on motorcycles who would terrorize the landscape, taking anything Drescher wanted, killing anyone who opposed him and recruiting everyone ambitious and ruthless enough into his dark army.

Sweet.

CHAPTER TWENTY

The thunderous roar of The Big Daddy's engines woke Drescher from his tyrannical daydream. Its high-beams froze him in his tracks, like a frightened deer.

The Dark Drivers scrambled in response to the threat. Their nervous systems were wired into their vehicles now, so they were literally as quick as the speed of thought.

The Big Daddy was faster.

Drescher bellowed with rage as Flynn and Krystal zoomed past him. The wind that rushed in to replace the air displaced by The Big Daddy toppled Drescher's bike and shook one of his fillings loose.

"Kill them, you idiots!" Drescher barked at his gang.

They complied, soaring after their target at a speed almost unfathomable to Krystal.

"I told you I had a plan" Flynn said jokingly.

Flynn's driving skills were still unparalleled. He was literally burning rubber—his tires had caught flame, but it didn't seem to have an adverse effect on his speed. He was still several car lengths ahead of Drescher's half-dead Dark Driver hounds.

Krystal was turned around in her seat, staring at The Dark Drivers and biting her lip.

Flynn reached over and caressed her leg.

"Hey—it's okay. Those goons don't have anything on us. They pretty much brought a 'smart car' to a Formula One competition...We've got absolutely nothing to worry about. We'll loose 'em, torch these creepy corpses, and everything will be right as rain. Trust me".

Krystal slapped his hand off her thigh.

"I'm not worried about them, you over confident

dork. I'm worried about him" she said, pointing at something off in the distance--but closing in closer with every second.

Flynn glanced over his shoulder, trying to get a glimpse at what she was talking about.

He saw.

And it wasn't pretty.

CHAPTER TWENTY-ONE

"If you want something done, you've got to do it yourself" Drescher muttered under his breath.

Case in point: his new strategy consisted of chasing down his own men and drive-by-consuming their essences and using their life force to boost his speed.

It was barbaric, and obscene, and unspeakably cruel—but it was effective. Very, very effective.

By Krystal's count Drescher was on his eighth guy. Their bodies lay scattered along the highway like fresh roadkill.

Drescher changed with each absorption. His shoulders grew broader. The wheels on his bike gained mass and sprouted cement-obliterating spikes. The faces of his victims manifested in the thick, obsidian smog his exhaust pipes spewed out.

"Umm...can you do me a solid and make sure your seat belt is secured?" Flynn asked Krystal. He was trying to play it cool, but his voice cracked just a little when he said the word "solid". It was embarrassing.

"Sure..." Krystal complied.

Flynn looked over and made sure she did.

"Rrrrrr!" the sound of The Big Daddy's wheels screeching to a complete stop was like nothing Krystal had ever heard. It was like the wailing of a dying animal, if that animal were a dying t-rex with the lungs of a pop diva.

As soon as she had recovered enough of her senses to think to question why they had stopped Flynn reached over, unfastened her seat belt, opened her door (with his mind, apparently), and shoved her out the car and she rolled out of sight into a dry riverbed.

"What are you doing, you impulsive, self-centered, over confident megalomaniac?" Krystal wanted to yell at him...but all that came out was a weak "Yeah, whu-huh?", before he closed his door and rocketed out of there like a firework on the Fourth of July.

"Get rid of all the dead weight you want, pretender! The real Road Rager is still comin' for ya!" Drescher yelled, his voice as loud as thunder.

Flynn exhaled. Drescher had driven right past Krystal. She was safe.

...Unless Flynn messed this next part up. Then nobody on Earth was.

CHAPTER TWENTY-TWO

Initially, Flynn thought that he was going to have to let Drescher catch up to him for the next part of his plant to work.

...That looked like it wasn't going to be a problem.

"I'm gonna eat your soul, boy! I'm gonna eat your soul, and I'm gonna use your precious car for scrap!" Drescher taunted Flynn, nipping at his heels.

Somehow the former seemed to be less scary than the latter. Flynn swore to himself that if he survived this gambit he was going to sit down with a nice therapist, or at least a halfway decent school counselor, and set his priorities nice and straight.

"Big talk, chump!" Flynn quipped...and then realized that his window was rolled all the way up. He rolled it down and repeated himself: "Big talk, chump!".

That "chump" part was a nice touch, Flynn thought to himself.

Drescher responded by ramming his vehicle into the driver's side of Flynn's car.

"I've been looking forward to seeing you again and finishing what we started!"

"I'm glad you feel that way" Flynn said, reaching out the window and grabbing hold of Drescher's bike.

"What are you doin'? " Drescher asked, a little confused.

Flynn didn't say a word. He answered Drescher's question by handcuffing himself to the bike with some cuffs taken from the police bag.

"Let me go, you lunatic!" Drescher growled, frustrated.

"Let yourself go, big shot" Flynn replied. "If you think you're faster than I am, then prove it. Or are you scared to really see what you're capable of...?"

They got to going so fast that they didn't even recognize the landscape anymore. Instead of buildings, trees, cars, billboards, everything was just one big blur—a kaleidoscope of colors and indefinable shapes that made Flynn's head hurt to look at. Drescher didn't seem to be doing much better.

But they both pressed on. They drove so fast they broke through the barrier that keeps the world of magic and material, gods and men, separate. They weren't just moving fast, they were the idea of "fast". They became Motion incarnate.

"I'm not scared of anything, kid...especially of you. I have this baby opened all the way up."

"That's great news..." Flynn said, smirking, "...but not for you"

With that, Flynn put the pedal down...all the way down.

...and the universes exploded around them.

CHAPTER TWENTY-THREE

Krystal's butt hurt. How dare that boy push her out of a car and on to her buns in the middle of the gosh dang road, in the middle of the dirty concrete reservoir? Who does that? What was his problem?

She swore right then and there that if she ever saw that Flynn again that she would kick his booty so hard the discomfort she felt right now wouldn't even compare. She'd kick his butt until her shoe came off—and then she'd make him buy her a brand new shoe—two brand new shoes! That's how much trouble he was in!

"Flynn..." she sighed, not knowing what else to do.

Suddenly, a hand appeared on her shoulder.

"Alright, already. I get it—I'm not the sharpest tool in the shed. But have you ever seen me behind the wheel...?"

It was Flynn! He was alive! He still had on the police gear stuff he picked up back at the station (but, frankly, that wasn't a problem--he looked danged handsome in it)--but the bandages, and the grisly runes they had covered, were completely gone!

"Your markings!", Krystal shouted, "Where'd they go?". She knew that she sounded like a complete doofus, but she didn't care. She was too happy to care.

Flynn smiled.

"They're still there..." he said, cryptically, "just...underneath the skin, now. It's sort of hard to explain..." he said. "Lemme tell you: I took a pretty weird trip, back there".

Krystal hugged him as hard as she was capable.

"I don't care where you've been" she said, "just so long as you're back...you big idiot".

Flynn hugged her back.

"But, while we're on the subject..." Krystal said, lingering off at the end and prompting him to fill in the blanks.

"I can't really articulate it too well, y'know", Flynn said. "Did you ever play with toy cars when you were a kid? On those little, orange, plastic tracks? Remember when you got 'em goin' so fast that they'd just shoot off the track and go flying across the room—into an army man scene you had set up across the room, or in between the couch cushions or whatever? That's what it was like—like I went off the tracks and wound up somewhere we weren't supposed to be, in some other scene. And we saw the world for what it was—from a, like, non-linear perspective. I saw stuff from outside the context of space and time and realized that things didn't occur in a straight line. That it's all just an illusion. And that made racing seem...stupid. I mean, my memory of this place is fading fast now but..."

"Were you the only ones there?" Krystal asked.

"No we... Drescher wasn't there...he couldn't keep up....he ended up...somewhere else...a place

102

that was all too happy to see him" Flynn finally said. "Where I ended up there were loads of other people there. People who had become untethered to their illusions of reality, too..."

"Like, dead people?" Krystal asked.

Flynn nodded.

Flynn punched Krystal playfully in the arm.

"Hey, good news though! All of the souls Drescher devoured when he was doing his 'Dracula' thing should have returned back to their bodies by now—so that means your Uncle Lassiter and my pops are back among the living. They're probably swapping baby photos of us right now..."

Krystal and Flynn both laughed for a minute—but then they realized that Flynn's statement was probably accurate, and then stopped on a dime.

They both took off running in the direction of The Big Daddy (which had reemerged shortly after Flynn had—back to its original, charming form) eager to see the folks who had made this evening one they wouldn't forget.

"This time, I'm driving!" Krystal shouted.

Flynn smiled. For the first time in his life he felt

like taking a break from driving for a while might not be so terrible an idea...

ABOUT THE AUTHOR

Eric M. Esquivel is a native of sunny Tucson, Arizona. This recently transposed Los Angeles based author, graphic novelist, screen writer, and journalist is making the most of his transition to the West coast. Eric's previous all ages stories include tales set in the *Adventure Time, Bravest Warriors, BOO!* and *Girl Scouts In Space* universes and look for more upcoming Actionopolis books from him in the future.

ABOUT THE CREATOR

Shannon Eric Denton is an award winning storyteller. Shannon created ACTIONOPOLIS to actualize his ideas into a line of fast paced books for adventure lovers of any age. He has been fortunate to have worked professionally as an artist, writer, editor, director, and producer making comic books, children's books, Emmy nominated TV shows, Oscar nominated movies, toys and video games for studios such as Marvel, DC, Disney, WB, Fox, Lego, Sony, Nickelodeon, and Cartoon Network.

www.shannondenton.com
www.actionopolis.com
www.agentofdanger.com

ACTIONOPOLIS:
When Adventure Is Your Destination!

Other books from
ACTIONOPOLIS & AGENT of D.A.N.G.E.R.

- Sword of the Seas
- Toltec
- ThunderBreakers
- Upgrader 2
- Valkyra
- Vampirium
- What I Did On My Hypergalactic Interstellar Summer Vacation
- White Knight
- Winged Victory
- Wonderworld
- Zombie Monkey Monster Jamboree

And Many More Titles Coming Soon!

A multitude of Adventures await!
Available as either physical manifestations...
a printed masterpiece on paper...or as a
program in the matrix for the technologically
advanced who prefer a digital eBook format!
You can find all the Actionopolis titles in print
or available on your preferred
eReading device!

WWW.ACTIONOPOLIS.COM

www.ingramcontent.com/pod-product-compliance
Lightning Source LLC
Chambersburg PA
CBHW070458130626
46555CB00003B/1053